P9-CLZ-675

Birthday Pony

BY JESSIE HAAS
PICTURES BY MARGOT APPLE

Greenwillow Books
An Imprint of HarperCollins*Publishers*

Birthday Pony

Printed in the United States of America. For information address HarperCollins Children's Books, a division of HarperCollins Publishers, 1350 Avenue of the Americas, New York, NY 10019.
www.harperchildrens.com

The text of this book is set in Schneidler.
Book design by Sylvie Le Floc'h

Library of Congress Cataloging-in-Publication Data
Haas, Jessie.
Birthday Pony / by Jessie Haas.
p. cm.
"Greenwillow Books."
Summary: Grandma Aggie tries to help her granddaughter Jane and the independent pony Popcorn, who were born on the same day, become riding partners.
ISBN 0-06-057359-7 (trade). ISBN 0-06-057360-0 (lib. bdg.)
[1. Ponies—Fiction. 2. Horsemanship—Fiction.
3. Grandmothers—Fiction.] I. Title.
PZ7.H11133Bi 2003 [Fic]—dc22 2003057286

First Edition 10 9 8 7 6 5 4 3 2 1

Greenwillow Books

For Michael, Jean Shaw,

and, especially, Cynthia Stowe

—J. H.

CONTENTS

CHAPTER ONE

Popcorn

Popcorn and Jane were born the same day, many miles apart. Popcorn was a pony foal who belonged to Grandma Aggie. Jane was Grandma Aggie's grandchild.

Popcorn grew faster than Jane did. When Jane could walk, Popcorn could gallop. When Jane was playing hopscotch, Popcorn was hopping over Grandma Aggie's pasture fence. Before Jane even started kindergarten, Popcorn went to the pony trainer.

The trainer taught Popcorn good manners. She taught him to let himself be ridden. It wasn't always easy.

"Popcorn is a great pony," the trainer told Grandma Aggie. "But he does like to get his own way. He'll need a good rider."

Ever since they were born, Grandma Aggie wanted Popcorn to be Jane's pony. But Jane was small and far away. She had never ridden a pony. Popcorn needed a rider soon.

So Grandma Aggie put an ad in the paper, and a family bought Popcorn for their little girl, Cathleen.

Cathleen was a good rider. She sat straight in the saddle. She kept her heels down and her head high. She even won ribbons at shows, riding one of the lesson ponies.

Popcorn liked Cathleen. She gave him carrots. She cleaned his stall every day. And with Cathleen, Popcorn always got his own way. Whatever Popcorn wanted to do, Cathleen let him do. She couldn't help it.

Cathleen's mother bought her books about training ponies. She sent her for more riding lessons. Still, Cathleen couldn't make Popcorn go where she wanted him

to go. She couldn't make him go slow when he wanted to go fast.

"They are a little too young for each other," Cathleen's riding teacher said. "Things will get better in a year or two."

Then, on Cathleen's birthday, her aunt gave her a mountain bike.

The bike went just where Cathleen pointed it. It went as fast as she wanted, and no faster. It didn't jump over anything.

Cathleen went biking after school. She went biking on weekends. She went biking all summer, and all the next summer, too.

Popcorn stayed in the pasture by himself. He ate grass. He ran races with the birds. When Cathleen biked past with her friends, Popcorn raced them, too. He always won. But the bikes went on beyond the pasture fence. Popcorn jumped the fence a few times. Cathleen's father made it higher.

Cathleen still fed Popcorn and watered him and took good care of him. She still rode him once in a while. But each summer she rode him less.

"I'm sorry for that pony," Cathleen's mother said. "Nothing to do, and nobody to do it with."

"I'm sorry for him, too," said Cathleen's father.

CHAPTER TWO

SweetPea

Far away, Jane rode the stick horse Grandma Aggie sent her. She rode the merry-go-round in the park. She rode the back of the couch. She even rode the dog.

Grandma Aggie visited every year on Jane's birthday. She brought Jane horse books. She brought horse models and horse posters and horse videos. The rest of the year she sent letters. She sent pictures of Popcorn's mother, SweetPea, too.

SweetPea was old. Once in a while Grandma Aggie saddled her and took a slow ride. The next day she and SweetPea were always stiff and sore. "Rode SweetPea to the mailbox," Grandma Aggie wrote to Jane. "Both of us are worn out."

Jane put the pictures on her wall. She dreamed of the day she would visit Grandma Aggie and ride SweetPea all the way to the mailbox.

When Jane was nine, her father got the job he'd always wanted. It was near where Grandma Aggie lived. They packed the couch, the stick horse, the dog, and everything else they owned and drove across the country to Grandma Aggie's house.

Jane and Grandma Aggie hugged

and kissed. Then Grandma Aggie said, "Come meet SweetPea!"

SweetPea was as white as a snowman. Her belly was round. Her hips had corners. Her back sagged in the middle.

"She looks older than in her pictures," Jane said.

"Not too old to give you riding lessons," Grandma Aggie said.

"The mailbox is closer to the house than I thought it would be," Jane said.

"It seems far away to me and

SweetPea," Grandma Aggie said. "We'll have short lessons at first, Jane, while SweetPea gets in shape."

Jane and her parents got a house of their own, but Jane spent every minute she could with Grandma Aggie and SweetPea.

Grandma Aggie taught Jane to sit tall in the saddle. She taught her to keep her heels down and her head high.

SweetPea taught Jane other

things. She taught her to let go of the reins when a pony eats grass. If Jane didn't let go, she slid down SweetPea's neck.

SweetPea taught Jane not to hurt her feelings. SweetPea's feelings were hurt if Jane didn't bring treats—lots and lots and lots of treats.

SweetPea taught Jane that sitting on an old pony or a tired pony or a grazing pony or even a sleeping pony is better than not sitting on a pony at all.

On rainy afternoons Grandma

Aggie told stories about when she and SweetPea were younger and thinner and faster. She showed Jane the ribbons they had won. She showed her pictures of SweetPea's foals—Pansy, Petunia, Peony, and Popcorn.

"Popcorn is the prettiest," Jane said.

"Pretty is as pretty does," said Grandma Aggie. "He was the wildest of the lot, and SweetPea spoiled him rotten."

"How?"

"She always let him have his own way. He jumped over her sometimes when she was lying down. He even pulled her tail. She bit the other three if they sassed her, but not Popcorn."

"Where are they now?" asked Jane.

"Pansy, Petunia, and Peony live on a pony farm. They have babies of their own. Popcorn belongs to a little girl. I loved them, but a slow old lady doesn't need a quick young pony."

"*I* do," Jane said.

"I know you do," said Grandma Aggie.

CHAPTER THREE

Happy Birthday

Winter came, and spring. Cathleen started biking again.

One day her father said, "I'd like to plant raspberries where the pony has his pasture."

"Where will Popcorn live?" Cathleen asked.

"I've been meaning to talk to you about that," said her father.

It was spring at Grandma Aggie's house, too. SweetPea's long hair came off like a snowstorm—all over the grass, all over Jane.

Jane started riding again. She hardly ever slid down SweetPea's neck anymore. Sometimes she could keep SweetPea from stopping to eat in the first place. She could ride to the mailbox by herself, and she could ride in the woods.

The only thing Jane could not do was make SweetPea go fast.

"I don't know if she can't or if she won't," said Grandma Aggie. "But she is an old pony and a good pony. Don't you get mad at her, Jane."

Jane knew SweetPea couldn't help being old. But now that she could ride by herself, she didn't want to walk slowly. She didn't want to go around logs on the trail.

Jane wanted to go fast. She wanted to jump.

Jane's birthday was on a Saturday.

"Let's have a family party at my house," Grandma Aggie said. "That way SweetPea can come."

Jane made a list of the presents she would like.

"No pony on the list?" Jane's mother asked. "You always ask for a pony."

"I don't want to hurt SweetPea's feelings," Jane said.

"I'm glad to hear that!" said Grandma Aggie.

Grandma Aggie came out of the house when Jane and her parents got there. She carried a cake. The cake had tiny carrots on top instead of candles.
"Twenty?" Jane said. "I'm only ten!"

"Come out to the barn," said Grandma Aggie.

Jane opened the door. A pony whinnied. SweetPea looked over her stall door. It was not SweetPea who had whinnied.

The other stall door had a big bow on it. A pony looked out. He was white and pretty and very loud.

"Happy birthday, Jane!" said Grandma Aggie. "And happy birthday, Popcorn! Finally you belong to each other."

Jane couldn't say anything, not even thank you. She just stared at Popcorn. Popcorn stared back. Then he whinnied to SweetPea again.

"The girl didn't ride him much," Grandma Aggie said. "She fell in love with mountain biking. They were just about to put him up for sale when I called to see if I could buy him back."

"Can I ride him?" Jane asked. She could whisper now, just barely.

"Not today," said Grandma Aggie. "Let's give him time to settle down."

Jane had her birthday cake in the barn. She gave the carrots to the ponies—ten to Popcorn and ten to SweetPea. She stood in front of Popcorn's stall and looked at him. Every few minutes she ran to pat SweetPea, so SweetPea's feelings would not be hurt.

"Looks like I'd better serve supper out here, too!" said Grandma Aggie.

After supper Jane's parents went home. Jane helped Grandma Aggie feed the ponies. She hugged SweetPea, and she patted Popcorn. "He's too wiggly to hug," she told Grandma Aggie.

"He's excited to be back home. He'll calm down in a day or two." Grandma Aggie turned out the light and closed the barn door.

"I think Popcorn will be a good pony for you," she said to Jane.

"He's young and quick, and he always liked to—"

Behind them in the barn something banged. Something scraped and scrambled and thudded.

Jane opened the door, and turned on the light.

Popcorn was stuck halfway over his door. His front feet scrabbled. His back feet waved in the air.

"—jump," Grandma Aggie said. Her eyes were as big as cake plates. "He always liked to jump."

"What should we do?" Jane asked.

"I don't think so," said Grandma Aggie. "Falling must have scared him a little."

But nothing scared Popcorn. In the morning both ponies were in SweetPea's stall.

Jane led SweetPea out to the pasture. Grandma Aggie led Popcorn. "Just this once, so I can see how he behaves. Slow down!" she said to Popcorn. "Ouch! Don't step on my foot."

"Maybe I should lead him," Jane said.

"You're not quite strong enough," Grandma Aggie said. "And I'm not fast enough!"

They let the ponies loose. SweetPea ate grass. Popcorn galloped. He jumped the brook. He pranced around SweetPea and tried to make her run, too. She did, for a few steps. Then she ate grass again.

"Soon," Jane whispered. Soon she would gallop along the trails on Popcorn. They would jump over every log they came to. And SweetPea could eat and rest all day long.

"Breakfast time," said Grandma Aggie. "Do you want French toast?"

"Yes!" Jane said.

They started toward the house. Behind them something thundered and rumbled and thumped. It was Popcorn galloping to the fence and hopping over it.

"He's such a great jumper!" Jane said.

"Wonderful!" said Grandma Aggie. She sounded tired. "We'd better put them back in the barn, Jane. And after breakfast we'll make that fence higher!"

CHAPTER FOUR

Trouble

All morning Jane and Grandma Aggie worked on the fence. After lunch Grandma Aggie took a nap. Finally it was time to ride Popcorn.

Jane put the saddle on.

Popcorn knew what to do about saddles. He took a big breath. His belly got much rounder.

Jane didn't notice. She pulled the girth tight. When Jane turned away, Popcorn let his breath out. Now the girth felt loose and comfortable.

Jane put the bridle on. Grandma Aggie snapped a long rope onto the bridle. She led Popcorn out to the pasture.

Jane tried to get on. The saddle slid down Popcorn's side, and—

whump!—Jane landed on her back.

"So you know that trick!" Grandma Aggie said. She explained to Jane what had happened, and they put the saddle back where it belonged. Jane tightened the girth. She waited for Popcorn to let his breath out. Then she tightened the girth again. This time when Jane mounted, the saddle didn't slip. Jane was on Popcorn for the first time ever.

It felt different. Popcorn didn't even stand still the way SweetPea did. He stood still in a wiggly, lively way. It felt as if something were going to happen.

"Walk him in a circle around me," Grandma Aggie said.

Popcorn pranced. He jigged. He bounced, and he frisked. No matter how hard Jane and Grandma Aggie tried, he did not walk.

"Maybe tomorrow he'll be calmer," Grandma Aggie said.

But Popcorn wouldn't walk the next day, or the next. "He doesn't like to walk," Jane said.

"He should do what you ask," Grandma Aggie said, "whether he likes it or not."

"He's tired of circles," Jane said. "Like me."

Grandma Aggie said, "Try riding him around the pasture." She unsnapped the rope.

Popcorn knew that he was free. He galloped across the pasture. He leaped over the brook. He skipped and skittered and danced.

When Popcorn stopped, Jane wasn't on him anymore. She was

sitting on the ground. Grandma Aggie bent over her.

Popcorn galloped back. He put his head down to see what Jane was doing.

Jane patted him. "I just wasn't ready," she told Grandma Aggie. She got back on.

Popcorn galloped away again. He jumped the brook. Jane splashed down behind him. Popcorn turned and looked at her.

"Are you okay?" asked Grandma Aggie. "Then hop back on!"

"I'm wet!" Jane said.

"Do you want a wet *walk* back to the barn," Grandma Aggie asked, "or a wet ride?"

She helped Jane mount. She led Popcorn to the barn.

"That's enough for one day," she said. "Tomorrow you'll do better."

The next day Jane fell off three times. The day after she fell off five times.

Popcorn didn't mean to make her fall. He didn't mind letting Jane sit on him. He just kept doing whatever he wanted. He ran so fast his tail streamed out behind him. He listened to his hooves drumming the ground. He jumped over puddles, sticks, the brook, and even his own shadow. Sometimes Jane stayed on. Sometimes she didn't. Either way she was no trouble at all to Popcorn.

Jane didn't get scared. She got mad. She cried sometimes, she was so mad. She wanted to gallop and jump. But she wanted to stay on, too. She wanted to decide which way they went. She wanted to decide if they went fast or slow.

Most of all, she wanted to ride in the woods.

Grandma Aggie said, “No. Not until Popcorn will do what you tell him.”

Jane tried harder. She learned to hang on tight. She learned when to let go. She learned to land on her feet.

She didn’t learn one thing about making Popcorn slow down.

“I can see why that girl didn’t ride him!” Grandma Aggie said. She called Popcorn’s trainer on the telephone.

"Sounds like he's gotten his own way too much," the trainer said. "Why don't you make a small ring for Jane to ride him in?"

So Grandma Aggie and Jane made a ring in one corner of the pasture. There was no room to go fast. There was nothing to jump. In the ring Popcorn walked. He trotted slowly. Once he even cantered; that's galloping, only slower. Jane had never gotten SweetPea to canter. She'd never gotten Popcorn to canter either.

In the ring Jane did not fall off.

She and Popcorn went around and around, around and around. Jane looked over the ring fence at the wide pasture and the wide woods.

One day Jane saw a poster in the grain store. There was going to be a horse show. It was nearby. It was small. "Could I take Popcorn?" she asked Grandma Aggie. "We'd be inside a ring."

"It might be too exciting for Popcorn," Grandma Aggie said. "But I'm tired of saying no to you. Let's try it."

CHAPTER FIVE

Show Pony

SweetPea came to the horse show, too. “To help Popcorn stay calm,” said Grandma Aggie.

But Popcorn didn’t stay calm. He whinnied and whirled and pranced.

Jane could hardly get his bridle on.

Grandma Aggie led them to the ring. "I hope this is a good idea," she said.

"Walk," said the ringmaster.

Popcorn trotted.

"Trot," said the ringmaster.

Popcorn galloped. He passed the other ponies, once, twice, three times. He wouldn't stop, no matter what Jane did.

Grandma Aggie came to help. Other people came, too. One woman had a grain bucket.

Popcorn stopped to see what was in it.

"Got you!" said Grandma Aggie. She led Popcorn and Jane back to the trailer. She took off the saddle and bridle. She put them on SweetPea.

"Ride in the next class," she told Jane. "It will make you feel better."

Jane didn't think anything could make her feel better. She got on SweetPea. She rode toward the ring. "Don't think about Popcorn!" Grandma Aggie said.

Jane couldn't help thinking about Popcorn. He was very loud.

But when SweetPea walked into the ring, she remembered that she was a show pony. Her head came up. Her eyes got bright. The ringmaster said, "Trot." SweetPea stretched her stiff old legs. She didn't trot fast, but she didn't trot slowly either.

"Canter," said the ringmaster.

SweetPea cantered.

Jane almost fell off from surprise. It was a rumbly, stumbly canter, and SweetPea couldn't keep it up for long. But the next time the ringmaster asked them to canter, SweetPea tried again.

"SweetPea, I love you," Jane said.

The judge gave SweetPea and Jane a ribbon. It wasn't first prize; that went to a girl named Rachel, on a little red pony named Radish. It wasn't second or third or fourth. It was fifth prize. The ribbon was pink, and it fluttered on SweetPea's bridle.

Jane rode back to the trailer. Grandma Aggie said, "Look at you two! You have stars in your eyes!"

JUDGE

Jane washed SweetPea with warm water. Grandma Aggie rubbed her legs. They talked about how good SweetPea was.

But soon they talked less, and then they didn't say anything for a while.

"What are we going to do about Popcorn?" Jane asked at last.

Grandma Aggie shook her head. "I don't know, Jane. I'm afraid he's just too much for us."

Jane sat looking at Popcorn until he went all shimmery. Then she hugged his neck. Popcorn blew his tickly breath on Jane's back. He always liked a hug from Jane.

"Hello," someone said behind them. It was the woman who had helped catch Popcorn. "What great ponies! But it looks to me like you could use some help."

"We certainly could!" said Grandma Aggie. "SweetPea and I taught Jane to ride, but we can't teach her to ride Popcorn!"

"SweetPea is too good," the woman said.

"And Popcorn is too bad!" said Grandma Aggie.

"Not bad, exactly," the woman said. "He just doesn't pay attention. And, Jane, you aren't a good enough rider yet to make him. But that can be fixed. My name is Tish. I have a riding camp. Some of my students and ponies were in the ring with you."

"Rachel?" Jane asked. "And Radish?"

"Yes," said Tish. "Rachel is going away for a month, so Radish won't have a rider. Why don't you both come to my camp? Radish can teach Jane, and my big boys and girls can teach Popcorn."

"*Can* they?" Grandma Aggie asked. "You saw what he's like."

Tish laughed. "They all were taught by Radish," she said. "They all are brave. They all are patient. They will know just what to do."

CHAPTER SIX

Radish

SweetPea went home with Jane and Grandma Aggie. She had bran mash and a soft bed and a good night's sleep.

Popcorn went to Tish's camp

with Radish and the other ponies. Tish put him in a stall of his own. Then she put him back in and closed the top door.

In the morning Jane came for her lesson. Grandma Aggie came, too, with her lawn chair and her knitting.

"Radish is an old pony, like SweetPea," Tish told Jane. "But he's not good like SweetPea. Radish is a good *bad* pony."

"What do you mean?"

"When you learn to ask him right, Radish will do what you want—

mostly. Until then he'll do what *he* wants."

Radish was used to getting new riders. They were always small. They were always scared of him, just a little.

Jane was bigger than most of Radish's riders. And Jane wasn't scared.

Radish didn't mind that. Jane was big, and Jane was brave, but Radish knew she couldn't make him do anything.

Jane asked Radish to walk. She expected him to gallop.

Radish did.

Jane asked him to stop. She knew he would keep going.

Radish didn't. It was Jane who kept going.

Jane was sure Radish wouldn't turn, not when he was trotting fast.

Radish did turn. Jane went straight.

"I fall off when he *does* what I ask just as much as when he doesn't!" Jane said.

"That's Radish for you," Tish said. "You have to expect him to do what

you ask. You have to be ready if he doesn't."

"I'm just glad he's small," said Jane. "Falling off doesn't hurt so much!"

Now it was time for Popcorn's lesson. One by one Tish's big boys and girls rode him. They were a lot more trouble than Jane was. They were good riders. They were bossy. Popcorn had to do what they wanted.

Popcorn didn't like that. He

would rather get his own way. But Ginger just laughed when he tried to run away with her. Then she sat deep in the saddle and slowed him down.

Popcorn tried to buck Kevin off. Kevin yelled, "Yippee!" He pulled Popcorn's head up and made him trot.

When Popcorn jumped over the low spot in the fence, Michelle didn't fall. She said, "Wow!" and turned Popcorn around and jumped him back in again, and out again, and in again, while Tish got a board to fix the fence.

Afterward the three of them talked to Jane.

"Popcorn's an amazing jumper!"

"He's pretty wild, though."

"Weren't you scared to ride him, just a little?"

"No," Jane said. "I just want him to do what I ask sometimes."

"You're brave," Kevin said.

"And patient, too," said Michelle.

"As soon as you know a little more," Ginger said, "you and

Popcorn will be perfect for each other."

Every day for three weeks Grandma Aggie brought Jane to Tish's camp. Jane ran to hug Popcorn first. He was always glad to see her.

Then Jane rode Radish. Grandma Aggie sat by the ring and knitted. Her sweater grew bigger and bigger.

Radish taught Jane to be ready for anything. He taught her to think ahead. He taught her to be careful what she asked for. She might suddenly get it.

Soon Jane expected Radish to do what she wanted. If he didn't, she learned to try again, more carefully.

The better Jane rode, the more fun she and Radish had. They jumped. They played broom polo. They went on trail rides with the other campers. Radish always knew a shortcut.

Jane loved trail rides on Radish,

but she watched what Popcorn was doing, too.

Every day Kevin, Ginger, and Michelle rode Popcorn. They taught him to wait and listen. They taught him to pay attention.

Soon Popcorn began to like doing what they wanted. Sometimes they wanted the same thing he wanted. Sometimes they had interesting new ideas.

The better Popcorn behaved, the more fun he had. He jumped. He played broom polo. He went on trail rides with the other campers. Popcorn always found something extra to jump on a trail ride.

Popcorn loved trail rides with Kevin, Ginger, or Michelle, but he paid attention to where Jane and Radish were, too.

Then one day Tish said, "Jane, today you will ride Popcorn."

CHAPTER SEVEN

Home Again

Ride Popcorn? Jane almost didn't want to. What if she and Popcorn weren't ready? What if Popcorn wasn't as much fun as Radish?

But the month was almost over.

Rachel would be back next week. It was time to try.

Jane tightened Popcorn's girth. She waited and tightened it some more. She got on.

Popcorn felt big to Jane. Jane felt small and light to Popcorn.

"Walk," Tish said.

Jane asked.

Popcorn walked.

"Trot," Tish said.

Jane asked.

Popcorn trotted.

"Canter," Tish said.

Jane took a deep breath. She remembered everything she had learned. Gently she asked Popcorn to canter.

Popcorn cantered.

"Oh!" Jane said. "It's wonderful!"

Popcorn went a little faster. Now he was galloping. Tish said, "Slow him down."

Jane asked.

Popcorn didn't slow down.

"Expect that he will," Tish said. "Be ready if he doesn't."

Jane didn't expect to slow Popcorn

down. She had never slowed him down before.

But she remembered slowing Radish down. She remembered what it felt like when she did everything exactly right. She sat deeper. She gently tightened the reins.

Popcorn knew that feeling. Kevin, Ginger, and Michelle did that when they wanted him to slow down.

For just a moment longer, Popcorn listened to his hooves drumming the ground. He felt his tail streaming out behind him.

Then he cantered. He trotted. He walked, and stopped, and stood still.

Kevin, Ginger, and Michelle smiled at one another. Grandma Aggie hugged the big new sweater, and Jane hugged Popcorn.

"Good for you!" Tish said. "Good for *both* of you!"

"Thank you," Jane said to all of them. "And thank you, Radish!"

For the rest of the week Jane jumped on Popcorn. She played broom polo on Popcorn. Popcorn took her on trail rides, and Popcorn did what Jane asked, mostly. When he didn't, Jane asked again, and sometimes a third time. If she asked right and kept asking, Popcorn almost always did what she wanted.

Popcorn didn't mind doing what Jane asked. She liked to go fast. She liked to jump. Those were the same things Popcorn liked. Doing what Jane asked was as good as getting his own way. "See?" Ginger said. "You two are perfect for each other."

On Sunday Grandma Aggie came with the trailer and took Popcorn home. Out in the pasture SweetPea lifted her head. She whinnied at Popcorn. Popcorn whinnied back.

Jane led Popcorn to the pasture and let him loose. Popcorn and SweetPea sniffed noses. They scratched each other's necks. Popcorn took a gallop around the field. Then he and SweetPea ate grass, side by side.

Monday afternoon Jane saddled Popcorn. Grandma Aggie saddled

SweetPea. Slowly they rode to the mailbox. Grandma Aggie got her mail. Slowly they rode back.

"Now you youngsters go have fun," said Grandma Aggie. She put SweetPea in the pasture. She sat on the porch to read her letters.

Jane rode Popcorn into the woods. They cantered along the trail. They splashed through the brook. They jumped over fallen logs and stone walls and shadows and a blueberry bush.

Then, slowly, but not too slowly, they came home again.